THE LOUD HOUSE

#10 "THE MANY FACES OF LINCOLN LOUD"

PAPERCUTZ™
New York

THE LOUD HOUSE

#10 "THE MANY FACES OF LINCOLN LOUD"

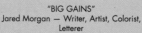

"THE HAUNTED HOUSE"
Derek Fridolfs — Writer
Max Alley — Artist
Amanda Rynda — Colorist
Wilson Ramos Jr. — Letterer

"TWINNING AT LIFE"
Caitlin Fein — Writer
Agny Innocente — Artist, Colorist
Wilson Ramos Jr. — Letterer

"LUCY OF MELANCHOLIA"
Caitlin Fein — Writer
Gizelle Orbino — Artist, Colorist
Wilson Ramos Jr. — Letterer

"MODEL BEHAVIOR"
Caitlin Fein — Writer
Erin Hyde — Artist, Colorist
Wilson Ramos Jr. — Letterer

"ROCKIN' ROUTINE"
Kiernan Sjursen-Lien — Writer
Lee-Roy Lahe — Artist
Hallie Lal — Colorist
Wilson Ramos Jr. — Letterer

"TERMS OF ENDEARMENT"
Jared Morgan — Writer, Artist, Colorist, Letterer

"NONE CHUCKED"
Derek Fridolfs, Zazo Aguiar — Writers
Zazo Aguiar — Artist, Colorist
Wilson Ramos Jr. — Letterer

"BRACE FOR IT"
Derek Fridolfs — Writer
Kelsey Wooley — Artist, Colorist
Wilson Ramos Jr. — Letterer

"BIG GAINS"
Jared Morgan — Writer, Artist, Colorist, Letterer

"CANDY HUNTING AT HUNTINGTON MANOR"
Sammie Crowley — Writer
Ari Castleton — Artist
Gabrielle Dolbey — Colorist
Wilson Ramos Jr. — Letterer

COLTON DAVIS — Cover Artist
JORDAN ROSATO — Endpapers
JAMES SALERNO — Sr. Art Director/Nickelodeon
JAYJAY JACKSON — Design
SAMMIE CROWLEY, SEAN GANTKA, ANGELA ENTZMINGER, DANA CLUVERIUS, MOLLIE FREILICH, ASHLEY KLIMENT, AMANDA RYNDA,
SONIA CANO, JARED MORGAN, CAITLIN FEIN — Special Thanks
JEFF WHITMAN — Editor
JOAN HILTY — Editor/Nickelodeon
JIM SALICRUP
Editor-in-Chief

ISBN: 978-1-5458-0473-5 paperback edition
ISBN: 978-1-5458-0474-2 hardcover edition

Papercutz books may be purchased for business or promotional use. For information on bulk purchases please contact Macmillan Corporate and
Premium Sales Department at (800) 221-7945 x5442.

Printed in the United States
August 2020

Distributed by Macmillan
First Printing

MEET THE LOUD FAMILY

LINCOLN LOUD
THE MIDDLE CHILD (11)

At 11 years old, Lincoln is the middle child, with five older sisters and five younger sisters. He has learned that surviving the Loud household means staying a step ahead. He's the man with a plan, always coming up with a way to get what he wants or deal with a problem, even if things inevitably go wrong. Being the only boy comes with some perks. Lincoln gets his own room – even if it's just a converted linen closet. On the other hand, being the only boy also means he sometimes gets a little too much attention from his sisters. They mother him, tease him, and use him as the occasional lab rat or fashion show participant. Lincoln's sisters may drive him crazy, but he loves them and is always willing to help out if they need him.

LORI LOUD
THE OLDEST (17)

As the first-born child of the Loud Clan, Lori sees herself as the boss of all her siblings. She feels she's paved the way for them and deserves extra respect. Her signature traits are rolling her eyes, texting her boyfriend, Bobby, and literally saying "literally" all the time. Because she's the oldest and most experienced sibling, Lori can be a great ally, so it pays to stay on her good side, especially since she can drive.

LENI LOUD
THE FASHIONISTA (16)

Leni spends most of her time designing outfits and accessorizing. She always falls for Luan's pranks, and sometimes walks into walls when she's talking (she's not great at doing two things at once). Leni might be flighty, but she's the sweetest of the Loud siblings and truly has a heart of gold (even though she's pretty sure it's a heart of blood).

LUNA LOUD
THE ROCK STAR (15)

Luna is loud, boisterous and freewheeling, and her energy is always cranked to 11. She thinks about music so much that she even talks in song lyrics. On the off-chance she doesn't have her guitar with her, everything can and will be turned into a musical instrument. You can always count on Luna to help out, and she'll do most anything you ask, as long as you're okay with her supplying a rocking guitar accompaniment.

LUAN LOUD
THE JOKESTER (14)

Luan's a standup comedienne who provides a nonstop barrage of silly puns. She's big on prop comedy too – squirting flowers and whoopee cushions – so you have to be on your toes whenever she's around. She loves to pull pranks and is a really good ventriloquist – she is often found doing bits with her dummy, Mr. Coconuts. Luan never lets anything get her down; to her, laughter IS the best medicine.

MR COCONUTS

Luan Loud's wise-cracking dummy.

BITEY

FANGS

LYNN LOUD
THE ATHLETE (13)

Lynn is athletic and full of energy and is always looking for a teammate. With her, it's all sports all the time. She'll turn anything into a sport. Putting away eggs? Jump shot! Score! Cleaning up the eggs? Slap shot! Score! Lynn is very competitive, but despite her competitive nature, she always tries to just have a good time.

LUCY LOUD
THE EMO (8)

You can always count on Lucy to give the morbid point of view in any given situation. She is obsessed with all things spooky and dark – funerals, vampires, séances, and the like. She wears mostly black and writes moody poetry. She's usually quiet and keeps to herself. Lucy has a way of mysteriously appearing out of nowhere, and try as they might, her siblings never get used to this.

LOLA LOUD
THE BEAUTY QUEEN (6)

Lola could not be more different from her twin sister, Lana. She's a pageant powerhouse whose interests include glitter, photo shoots, and her own beautiful, beautiful face. But don't let her cute, gap-toothed smile fool you; underneath all the sugar and spice lurks a Machiavellian mastermind. Whatever Lola wants, Lola gets – or else. She's the eyes and ears of the household and never resists an opportunity to tattle on troublemakers. But if you stay on Lola's good side, you've got yourself a fierce ally – and a lifetime supply of free makeovers.

LANA LOUD
THE TOMBOY (6)

Lana is the rough-and-tumble sparkplug counterpart to her twin sister, Lola. She's all about reptiles, mud pies, and muffler repair. She's the resident Ms. Fix-it and is always ready to lend a hand – the dirtier the job, the better. Need your toilet unclogged? Snake fed? Back-zit popped? Lana's your gal. All she asks in return is a little A-B-C gum, or a handful of kibble (she often sneaks it from the dog bowl).

LISA LOUD
THE GENIUS (4)

Lisa is smarter than the rest of her siblings combined. She'll most likely be a rocket scientist, or a brain surgeon, or an evil genius who takes over the world. Lisa spends most of her time working in her lab (the family has gotten used to the explosions), and says her research leaves little time for frivolous human pursuits like "playing" or "getting haircuts." That said, she's always there to help with a homework question, or to explain why the sky is blue, or to point out the structural flaws in someone's pillow fort. Lisa says it's the least she can do for her favorite test subjects, er, siblings.

LILY LOUD
THE BABY (15 MONTHS)

Lily is a giggly, drooly, diaper-ditching free spirit, affectionately known as "the poop machine." You can't keep a nappy on this kid – she's like a teething Houdini. But even when Lily's running wild, dropping rancid diaper bombs, or drooling all over the remote, she always brings a smile to everyone's face (and a clothespin to their nose). Lily is everyone's favorite little buddy, and the whole family loves her unconditionally.

 CHARLES   **WALT**   **CLIFF**   **GEO**

RITA LOUD

Mother to the eleven Loud kids, Mom (Rita Loud) wears many different hats. She's a chauffeur, homework-checker and barf-cleaner-upper all rolled into one. She's always there for her kids and ready to jump into action during a crisis, whether it's a fight between the twins or Leni's missing shoe. When she's not chasing the kids around or at her day job as a dental hygienist for Dr. Feinstein, Mom pursues her passion: writing. She also loves taking on house projects and is very handy with tools (guess that's where Lana gets it from). Between writing, working and being a mom, her days are always hectic but she wouldn't have it any other way.

LYNN LOUD SR.

Dad (Lynn Loud Sr.) is a fun-loving, upbeat aspiring chef. A kid-at-heart, he's not above taking part in the kids' zany schemes. In addition to cooking, Dad loves his van, playing the cowbell and making puns. Before meeting Mom, Dad spent a semester in England and has been obsessed with British culture ever since – and sometimes "accidentally" slips into a British accent. When Dad's not wrangling the kids, he's pursuing his dream of opening his own restaurant where he hopes to make his "Lynn-sagnas" world-famous.

CLYDE McBRIDE
THE BEST FRIEND (11)

Clyde is Lincoln's partner in crime. He's always willing to go along with Lincoln's crazy schemes (even if he sees the flaws in them up-front). Lincoln and Clyde are two peas in a pod and share pretty much all of the same tastes in movies, comics, TV shows, toys—you name it. As an only child, Clyde envies Lincoln—how cool would it be to always have siblings around to talk to? But since Clyde spends so much time at the Loud household, he's almost an honorary sibling anyway.

RUSTY SPOKES

Rusty is a self-proclaimed ladies' man who's always the first to dish out girl advice—even though he's never been on an actual date. His dad owns a suit rental service, so occasionally Rusty can hook the gang up with some dapper duds—just as long as no one gets anything dirty.

ZACH GURDLE

Zach is a self-admitted nerd who's obsessed with aliens and conspiracy theories. He lives between a freeway and a circus, so the chaos of the Loud House doesn't faze him. He and Rusty occasionally butt heads, but deep down, it's all love.

LIAM

Liam is an enthusiastic, sweet-natured farm boy full of down-home wisdom. He loves hanging out with his Mee Maw, wrestling his prize pig Virginia, and sharing his farm-to-table produce with the rest of the gang.

STELLA

Stella, 11, is a quirky, carefree girl who's new to Royal Woods. She has tons of interests, like trying on wigs, playing laser tag, eating curly fries, and hanging with her friends. But what she loves the most is tech — she always wants to dismantle electronics and put them back together again.

SAM SHARP

SIMON SHARP

Sam, 15, is Luna's classmate and good friend, who Luna has a crush on. Sam is all about the music – she loves to play guitar and write and compose music. Her favorite genre is rock and roll but she appreciates all good tunes. Unlike Luna, Sam only has one brother, Simon, but she thinks even one sibling provides enough chaos for her.

LENI'S COWORKER FRIENDS

FIONA

MIGUEL

WUMPH

≈PSSST≈
...DID YOU HEAR THAT, CLYDE?

YEAH. I THINK YOUR HOUSE IS *HAUNTED, LINCOLN.*

ONLY ONE WAY TO FIND OUT.

CLINCOLN McCLOUD, *PARANORMAL INVESTIGATORS.*

MY ASSOCIATE, AGENT LOUD, HEARD SPOOKY SOUNDS.

YEAH! I HEARD SPOOKY SOUNDS. SAY, HAVE YOU SEEN ANY GHOSTS?

GO TO BED!

SLAM **SLAM** **SLAM**

THAT WOULD BE A NEGATIVE, AGENT McBRIDE.

KLINK BANG RATTE-RATTE

THERE IT IS AGAIN. FOLLOW THOSE SOUNDS!

IT'S COMING FROM UP THERE. YOU LOOK FIRST!

RINGGGG

‹GULP!› THINK IT'S AN ALIEN ABDUCTION?

THAT OR ‹GULP!› WE ARE BEING HAUNTED BY *GREGORY FARFUNKEL!**

SHUDDER

*SEE THE LOUD HOUSE #5 "AFTER DARK" FOR THE CHILLING TALE.

EEEEEEEK!

GLICK

RINGGGG

13

EEEEEEK!

OH, IT'S ONLY YOU TWO. THANKS FOR FINDING ME.

DAD, WHAT ARE YOU DOING UP HERE?

I'VE BEEN STUCK IN THIS ATTIC ALL EVENING. JUST TRYING TO FIND MY COLLECTION OF PRIZED COW BELLS.

IT APPEARS YOUR HOUSE ISN'T HAUNTED AFTER ALL.

RATTLE RATTLE

OLD TOYS

IT ALSO APPEARS THAT WE'RE NOW STUCK.

HEY! LET US OUUUUUT!

WUMPH WUMPH WUMPH

OOOO... DID YOU HEAR THAT? I THINK OUR HOUSE IS HAUNTED.

WUMPH WUMPH WUMPH

YOU KNOW WHAT THAT MEANS? IT'S GHOST HUNTING TIME!

BEST. NIGHT. EVER.

END

14

"LUCY OF MELANCHOLIA"

GRISELDA?

AND GRISELDA?

AND GRISELDA?

AW, NOTHING LIKE A QUIET NIGHT IN WITH MY FAVORITE TV SHOW: "VAMPIRES OF MELANCHOLIA."

EDWIN, IT'S NOT WHAT YOU THINK. I'M CURSED WITH A DEVASTATING SECRET. THE SECRET IS--

THE BURPIN' BURGER!

JEAN JUAN'S!

THE BURPIN' BURGER!

SIGH. I THOUGHT YOU WERE ALL GOING OUT TONIGHT?

CHILLAX, WE'RE LEAVING...

...ONCE THEY COME TO THEIR SENSES.

COME ON, DUDES!

YOU NEVER GO WITH MY PICK!

I NEED MY PROTEIN!

SIGH.

IT'S NOT EASY FOR A MODERN GOTH GIRL TO LIVE WITH SUCH A LIVELY FAMILY.

≒YAWN!≒ I WISH I LIVED SOMEWHERE DARK AND QUIET. SOMEWHERE LIKE.... LIKE...

ZZZZ.

LUCINDA! THE SUN SETS. IT'S TIME TO RISE.

FANGS, COULD IT BE?

COULD YOU KEEP YOUR VOLUME DOWN?

HERE IN MELANCHOLIA, WE LIKE TO USE OUR INSIDE VOICES...

I'M HOME.

THIS BOOK IS EVERYTHING.

SSSSH.

SHHHHH.

Modern Embalming Practices

UM, SORRY...

SHHHHH.

CAW!

SHHHHH.

COUGH!

DID YOU SAY SOMETHING?

SHAKE

SIGH. ALL THE GARLIC-FREE GARLIC BREAD IN THE WORLD COULDN'T LIVEN UP THIS DINNER...

FANGS, I NEVER THOUGHT I'D SAY THIS BUT...I WISH I WAS SOMEWHERE LOUDER.

YAWN!

YAWN!
I COULDN'T SAY IT BETTER MYSELF.

SNORE!

END

"ROCKIN' ROUTINE"

"NONE CHUCKED"

LISA NOW MAKES MORE SMOKE BOMBS THAN EVER BEFORE. LILY'S STINK BOMBS ARE TEN TIMES MORE LETHAL.

LENI CHANNELED HER INNER VISION FOR NINJA-WEAR, WITH HER SKILLFUL PROWESS, SHE CAN MAKE NINJA OUTFITS OUT OF ANYTHING.

I RAN OUT OF LUCY'S BED SPREAD.

LUNA GAINED THE POWER OF FURIOUS SOUND. THIS NINJA CAN MAKE SOME REAL NOISE.

I'M THE SHREDDER!

LYNN GOT A SUPREME TECHNIQUE FOR EXTRA-SPORTY NINJA EQUIPMENT!

LUAN LEARNED THE SACRED ART OF THE INFINITE KNOCK KNOCK JOKE. THEY KEEP KNOCKING, BUT YOU WILL NEVER LEARN WHO'S THERE...

LOLA AND LANA MASTERED THE ELEMENTS OF THE EARTH AND THE STARS.

BE IT GLITTER OR DIRT, THESE TWO KNOW HOW TO GET EVERYWHERE.

AND ME, I WAS ALWAYS AWESOME, SO WHY CHANGE LITERAL PERFECTION.

big gains

TODAY I'M HELPING LYNN WITH HER WORKOUT ROUTINE LEADING UP TO A BIG WRESTLING MATCH.

FIRST THOUGH, I'M MAKING HER SPECIAL PRE-WORKOUT SMOOTHIE!

WHIRRRR

28

FOLLOW ME!

?!

ZIP

LENI, WHAT GIVES?!

HERE YA GO!

PLOP

UGH! WHY'D YOU DRAG ME UP TO THE BATHROOM LINE?

HAHA HAHA

I THOUGHT YOU SAID YOU WANTED-- "MORE WAIT?"

END

WHOA! *LOLS,* CAN YOU BELIEVE HOW MANY PEOPLE SHOWED UP TO THE TWIN CONVENTION?

ROYAL WOODS WELCOMES TWINS!

AND ALL WEARING MATCHING OUTFITS, *LANS?* TWO WORDS: NO THANKS.

OOH, GIRLS, SHOULD WE GO TO THE LECTURE ON *TWIN TELEPATHY?* OR *DECONSTRUCTING DOPPLEGANGERS?*

UMMM...

WAIT! IT'S *SARA* AND *TARA* FROM MY FAVORITE SITCOM... *"HERE COMES DOUBLE!"*

OMGOSH!

OH, GREAT. MOM'S TURNING INTO *LENI!*

WANNA DIG THROUGH THIS BAD BOY? SEE IF THERE'S ANYTHING COOL?

SIGN UP NOW FOR THE CROWN JEWEL OF THE CONVENTION: THE "TWINSIEST TWIN COMPETITION"...

THERE! THAT! COOL!

NO WAY! I DON'T WANT OUR TWIN THING TO BE JUDGED!

PLEEEEESE? I'LL MAKE YOU A MUD PIE.

UGH, MY TIGHTS ARE RIDING UP. WHY COULDN'T WE WEAR MATCHING SWEATS? OR OOH! TRACK SUITS!

PLEASE, THE JUDGES ARE GONNA EAT THIS LOOK UP. NOW TO PRACTICE THE HARD PART.

HARD PART?

GIFT SHOP

HUH. MAYBE THERE IS NO HARD PART.

RIGHT? THIS TWIN THING IS TOTALLY NATURAL!

SLURP

SLURP

IYAY AVEHAY AINBRAY EEZEFRAY!

OH, NO! IT'S FINALLY HAPPENING. MUD BRAIN! DON'T LOOK INTO THE LIGHT.

NO, SILLY! I'M TRYING TO FORM OUR OWN SPECIAL TWIN LANGUAGE! DUH!

OH, WHAT'S TWIN FOR "YOU GOT SODA ON YOUR DRESS"?

ATTENTION TWINS! THE COMPETITION IS ABOUT TO START!

WHAT?!

THERE YOU TWO ARE! WHAT ARE YOU WEARING?

IT'S SHOWTIME!

HEY!

SPLASH

THANKS, SIS.

MMM. HMM. YOU TWO WANT TO TELL ME WHAT'S GOING ON?

OH, MOM... ⸓SIGH.⸓

WE WANT TO WIN THE TWINSIEST TWIN COMPETITION.

WE'RE SPEAKING IN UNISON!

GIRLS, THAT'S GREAT, AND QUITE FRANKLY A LITTLE UNNERVING BUT... YOU TWO SHOULDN'T TRY TO SEEM MORE ALIKE SO THAT YOU WIN A COMPETITION!

YOU SHOULD BE PROUD OF YOUR SIMILARITIES AND DIFFERENCES! YOU MAY SHARE SOME FEATURES, BUT THERE'S ONLY ONE LANA AND ONE LOLA! AND THAT'S PRETTY SPECIAL AS IS.

YOU'RE RIGHT, MOM. READY TO COMPETE AS OURSELVES, LOLS?

YEAH. LET'S WIN THIS!

ARE YOU READY TO ANNOUNCE THE CUTEST, TWINSIEST PAIR, SARA?

CAN IT BE US, TARA?!

HAHAHAHA!

GRRR! JUST PICK SOMEONE!

TARA AND SARA STILL GOT IT!

LOLA, SHH!

AND THE WINNER IS...

MOOCHIE AND MARLEY!

ARF! ARF!

⸰GRRRR⸰

EEK!

WELL, WE MAY NOT BE THE "TWINSIEST TWINS" BUT WE'RE NOT LEAVING EMPTY-HANDED.

YOU GOT THAT RIGHT!

WHERE DID YOU EVEN GET THAT?!

SERIOUSLY, HOW ARE WE EVEN *RELATED?*

NOM NOM NOM

TARA! SARA! CAN YOU SIGN MY SCRUNCHIE?

END

"MODEL BEHAVIOR"

HI, *MIGUEL, FIONA.* IS *LENI* OFF YET?

THIS LOOK IS SO *YOU, MR. GROUSE!* BUT I THINK IT'S FACING THE WRONG WAY.

⇕HUMPH.⇕ THEN WHY CALL IT A *FANNY PACK?*

SHE'LL BE DONE IN FIVE. ARE YOU HERE FOR YOUR SISTER SHOPPING DAY?

NOPE. I'M HERE FOR OUR *SUPER* SISTER SHOPPING DAY!

CUTE...

RIGHT?! WE HAVE SO MUCH PLANNED SINCE WE NEVER GET "JUST US" TIME AND--

I *LITERALLY* HAVE TO GET *BOBBY* THAT SWEATER!

PERF! MANNEQUIN DRESSED.

WE'VE EARNED OUR SMOOTHIE BREAK.

HEY, GIRL, LORI'S HERE!

DID YOU HEAR THAT, MR. GROUSE? IT'S TIME FOR SUPER SISTER SHOPPING DAY!

SUPER.

LORI? LORI?!

GASP!

≳AAH!≲ YOU'VE BEEN TURNED INTO A MANNEQUIN! I ALWAYS FEARED THIS DAY WOULD COME...

OH, WELL! AT LEAST, WE CAN STILL HAVE OUR MALL DAY.

DON'T YOU JUST LOVE THE HAND MASSAGE PART, LORI?

LIKE, I CAN'T WATCH!

WHICH DO YOU LIKE BETTER? CHERRY TERRIER OR SNICKERPOODLE?

CLONK

OMGOSH! I'M ALSO FALLING FOR BOTH! BEST SISTER DAY EVER!

@NAME:LENILOUD

CARLOTTA LIKES THIS

BEST SHOPPING DAY EVER #SUPERSISTER

THAT MANNEQUIN LITERALLY LOOKS JUST LIKE ME!

I'M REALLY NOT SURPRISED.

SLURP

BUT WHERE ARE THEY NOW?!

YOU TALKING ABOUT THAT BLONDE GIRL AND HER QUIET FRIEND?

SHE'S A MANNEQUIN.

I'M NOT HERE TO JUDGE, BUT I THINK THEY WERE HEADED TO THE PARKING LOT.

42

PRESS START

ALRIGHT! LET'S DO THIS!

TERMS AND CONDITIONS

HUH? "TERMS AND CONDITIONS"? UH, I THINK WE CAN JUST SKIP THIS PART--

NOOOOOOOOOOO!

LINCOLN! TERMS AND CONDITIONS ARE A VERY IMPORTANT PART OF LIVING IN THE DIGITAL AGE. YOU SHOULD ALWAYS CAREFULLY READ OVER WHATEVER USER AGREEMENTS YOU ENTER INTO. IT'S THE RESPONSIBLE THING TO DO!

AND BESIDES, READING IS FUN.

"BRACE FOR IT"

50

"CANDY HUNTING AT HUNTINGTON MANOR"

OKAY, GUYS! SO... THIS IS THE MAGICAL PLACE THAT GIVES OUT *FULL-SIZED* CANDY BARS.

HUNTINGTON MANOR! ARE YOU GUYS READY FOR THE BEST HALLOWEEN EVER?!

WOOO!

KNOCK
KNOCK
KNOCK

TRICK OR TREAT!

WHAT LOVELY COSTUMES!

BITE-SIZED CANDY?!

WHAT HAPPENED TO THIS PLACE, *LINC?!* WHERE ARE THE FULL-SIZE BARS?

I HOPE THEY DON'T THINK WE'RE TOO *OLD* TO BE TRICK-OR-TREATING, *LENI...*

DING DONG

OH, I SEE WE HAVE SOME "TEENS" OUT TONIGHT.

HEH. HEH.

TAKE *EXTRA!* YOU'RE GROWING!

OKAY, NOW DON'T FORGET, *LANA*...WE HAVE ANOTHER SET OF COSTUMES TO CHANGE INTO IF WE DON'T GET ENOUGH OUT OF THIS HOUSE.

DING DONG

TRICK OR TREAT!

WOOSH

I DON'T THINK WE'RE GOING TO BE NEEDING OUR COSTUME CHANGES, *LOLA*...

OKAY, LILY, LET'S MAKE SURE WE'RE PUTTING OUT MAXIMUM CUTENESS FOR MAXIMUM CANDY RETURN!

GOO!

DING DONG

TRICK OR TREAT!

ICK AME!

NAB

ON

CANDY BLASTER 5000

WELL, THIS TURNED OUT EVEN BETTER THAN I POSSIBLY COULD HAVE HYPOTHESIZED.

≒AHEM!≒

ARE YOU BOYS DONE YET? WE SHOULD *PROBABLY* GO HOME...

YOU'RE RIGHT, *LORI*, WE PROBABLY HAVE ENOUGH CANDY.

WATCH OUT FOR PAPERCUTZ

Welcome to the twinsiest tome yet—the tenth THE LOUD HOUSE graphic novel "The Many Faces of Lincoln Loud," from Papercutz, those multiple personalities dedicated to publishing great graphic novels for all ages. I'm Jim Salicrup, Editor-in-Chief and one of the two Gemini Papercutz business partners. Gemini is the zodiac sign of the Twins, and while Papercutz publisher Terry Nantier and I aren't actual twins, we were born four days apart, but we're about as different from each other as the twin Loud sisters. While you'll find a great Lola and Lana adventure in these pages, mostly we're celebrating all the other guises that Lincoln Loud takes on. From Ace Savvy to Clincoln McCloud, our man Linc takes role-playing to new heights!

You know, once when I was a kid I had a dual identity without even realizing it! A friend's mother thought I was two different people—once when I hadn't had a haircut for a while (I had long curly black hair back then) and then after I got a haircut (she liked the short-haired me best). Do you have a tale of two identities?.

In various other Papercutz graphic novels, dual identities are not all that uncommon. In THE MYTHICS #1 "Heroes Reborn," for example, we meet three kids from around the world who soon become super-powered incarnations of old powerful beings. Please, allow me to introduce them…

The god of lightning, Raijin, instills his powers in Yuko, a Japanese schoolgirl in a rock band. Yuko must learn to wield her newfound electrical powers to defeat Fuijin, the evil god of wind, before he destroys all of Japan.

Meanwhile, in Egypt, young Amir, a recently orphaned boy taking over his father's successful company and landholdings, encounters Horus, the Sun and Moon god. Horus and Amir must stop evil, in the form of Seth, from reanimating all the dead mummies and taking over the world.

Lastly, a young opera hopeful, Abigail, must face a blizzard freezing all of Germany orchestrated by Loki, the evil god of mischief. Under the guidance of Freyja, the Norse god of beauty, Abigail must find her voice and her mythic weapon to stop evil in its tracks.

You can meet all three in THE MYTHICS #1, available now wherever you get your graphic novels.

While the kids from THE MYTHICS literally turn into different beings, over in THE SISTERS, Maureen and Wendy often imagine themselves as having super powers and battling all kinds of villains and monsters. In fact, that part of the series proved to be so popular there's an entire SUPER SISTERS graphic novel devoted to new, longer versions of those imaginary adventures. It too, is available now at your favorite booksellers and libraries. And that's exactly where you'll soon find THE LOUD HOUSE #11, featuring more fun with Lincoln, his ten sisters, and all their friends and families. We're sure you won't want to miss it!

Thanks,

STAY IN TOUCH!

EMAIL: salicrup@papercutz.com
WEB: papercutz.com
TWITTER: @papercutzgn
INSTAGRAM: @papercutzgn
FACEBOOK: PAPERCUTZGRAPHICNOVELS
FANMAIL: Papercutz, 160 Broadway, Suite 700 East Wing, New York, NY 10038